Follow me on twitter **@Moon081471**
Instagram: Fanita Pendleton
Connect with me on Facebook **Fanita Moon Pendleton**
Website www.urbanmoonproductions.com
Join my Readers Group on Facebook... Fanita Moon
Pendleton's Readers
Please be sure to leave your review.

Reviews are important to authors they give you a voice, but they are also important to potential readers who want to know from someone who has read the book how they liked it. I appreciate your support............

MOET

Money Over Everything

BY FANITA MOON PENDLETON

This is a work of fiction. All of the characters, organizations, and events portrayed in this novel are either products of the author's imagination or are used fictitiously. Any resemblance to actual persons, living or dead, is purely coincidental.

Acknowledgments

My son is the light of my life. Helping him grow into a young man has been the single most important thing that I have ever done. I hope him witnessing me fulfill my dreams encourages him to shoot for his. I love you **Brione Lamont Pendleton**.

Family Shout Out's to my Oakland California Family, Norfolk Virginia Family, Oklahoma Family, Texas Family, New York Family, and Hopkinsville, Kentucky Family.

Special Shout Out to **Mig** for holding **Urban Moon Productions** down with his debut series, **Dirty Red: A Killa's Love Story**….. I love you man. Check out his work on Nook and Kindle. www.Urbanmoonproductions.com

Shout out to **Blaque Diamond Publications** TEAM Authors Shauntrell Perry, Jauwel, Meka, Roni J, K. L. Hall, Cinnamon Brown, Kieta B, Mimi Ray, Shanard Smith, and Chantel Sills. In the hard times you guys stood strong and for that I thank you guys from the bottom of my heart. **Let's Keep Dropping that Heat!!!!!!!!**

I want to thank you for being a part of my movement. A Special Shout Out goes to all the authors and readers who supported me by downloading, reading and reviewing my work.

Checking Out

The explosion took out half of the Las Vegas Boulevard exit. Fire and smoke were thick enough to turn the morning sky into night. The smell of burning flesh was heavy in the air and traffic was at a standstill as first responders attempted to keep the chaos to a minimum. The scene didn't resemble the Vegas that millions of people flocked to every year. Instead, it looked like the middle of Kuwait on a good day.

Moet stood in her living room trying to dial her husband back; they were just talking then the call dropped. She could hear the alert on the news as she managed the phone in one hand and the coffee pot in the other. The phone continued to go straight to voicemail. Shrugging it off, she continued to make her morning coffee while thinking about what she needed to accomplish before her husband and son returned from their Saturday morning boys' time. Reflecting on how special their father and son time together was made her feel good inside.

Saturday mornings was also her "me" time. Moet would have a lazy morning, drink coffee, and run errands. The ringing of her phone caused her to smile as she said, *About time*. Picking the phone up quickly, she answered in that sexy voice that her man loved,

"You miss big momma don't ya?"

There was a crackle on the line and sirens could be heard in the background, causing Moet to pull the phone from her ear and look at the screen; the screen read Ed Lover.

Rolling her eyes, Moet was shaking her head as she tried to understand what Ed was saying. Ed was her older cousin; they were tight but he was always into something and she was sure this morning was no exception as she said,

"Ed, I can't understand a word you're saying. You know you messing with my Saturday morning peace man."

The chaotic sounds cleared up then she could hear him clearer which made her smile a little. Moet loved her cousin and knew he would do anything for her when it came down to it.

Ed didn't want to believe what he just saw and was hoping that Killa and HJ were already back home safely. He knew it was Saturday morning father and son time, so when he saw the smoke grey Lamborghini getting off at exit 11, he already knew what time it was. Before he could turn his focus back to his own leisure Saturday morning drive, the entire exit blew the fuck up.

The entire section of the 215 beltway collapsed; the fire and smoke caused it look like the end of the world. Trying to remain calm, he said into the phone,

"Moet, tell me that Killa and HJ are home with you."

Picking up on the distress in her cousin's voice, the hairs on the back of her neck began to rise. Ed was a hood nigga, nothing affected him other than somebody fucking with his family or his money.

The mention of Killa and HJ were enough to alert her that some shit had gone down. Bracing herself with the counter, she replied,

"They're not here Ed; tell me what happened."

As she listened, she gripped the edge of the counter harder. She felt her world literally implode. Although she could hear Ed calling her name, she couldn't answer him; she had checked out.

Ten Years Earlier - Destiny

My Goodies by Ciara was blasting through the backyard of the modest, three bedroom, ranch house. All you could see from corner to corner were teenage girls backing that thang up and horny boys trying to cop a feel. The guest of honor sat in a comfortable lawn chair with her right-hand chicks, Marisha and Steph, taking it all in. They were all happy to finally be graduating from high school and even more excited to be going away to college. Moet had been through a lot in her young life. If it weren't for the strong relationship with Marisha and Ed, she would be ready to get away from Vegas. Instead, she chose the University of Nevada at Las Vegas (UNLV). She would stay on campus where she could still chill with her girls and outrun the ghosts of her past.

All of her friends were at the party even the ones who dropped out years before. Looking around, she smiled at the great job her aunt did decorating the backyard. The color scheme was red and white which are her favorites. As a centerpiece, each table had a white graduation cap with a red tassel hanging from it. All of the tablecloths were red and there were balloons that read congratulations everywhere. In one section of the large backyard, there were blackjack, roulette, spades, and domino tables crowded with laughter as real paper spread around. She knew her cousin had spared no expense to make sure she had the best graduation party that Vegas had seen in years.

The song switched to *Usher and Lil Jon* and the dance area got even more crowded. She noticed her so-called boyfriend approaching with that bop that all the fellas used when they were trying way too hard to look cool. Superb really didn't need the bop though. Watching him approach was like watching a young movie star or even model; he was just that fine. At 18-years-old, he was already a 5'11", light-skinned, heartthrob. She still couldn't believe he was interested in her. It wasn't as if she thought she looked bad or anything like that. In fact, she knew she had a little something going on. Moet and her girls stayed fly. They just didn't get down with a lot of bullshit. Moet was aware there were girls everywhere willing to put out for Superb. However, she didn't happen to be one of them.

Although she thought Superb was an ok dude, his problem was he assumed he was the best thing ever. Consequently, Moet wasn't sure how much longer she was going to put up with him. Besides, her heart just wasn't in it anymore. She still couldn't deny how fine he was though.

He stopped in front of her, wearing that sexy grin he always had when he looked at her and said,

"Moet, you gonna sit your sexy ass over here with the evil twins all night or you gonna dance with your man?"

Moet didn't feel like dancing with Superb even though she knew she was the envy of every girl there. It showed in the way they cut their eyes at her.

Therefore, she hurried up and got out of her chair before Marisha and Steph jumped on him. Neither of them liked Superb.

They called him a broke busta. Moet realized how wild it would get if she didn't separate them because her girls would not let up on his ass, and Moet didn't feel like hearing it. She also decided to give the gawkers something to look at, thinking if they want something to be mad about, let me give them a real good reason.

Wearing her red, Baby Phat, cropped pants that hugged every inch of her youthful curves with a matching top, she allowed Superb to pull her away from her crew. They were making small talk as they began to move their bodies to the beat. She noticed Superb appeared to be slightly intoxicated; he knew she hated drinking, but the music was so good she let it go. She decided to forget about all the chicks who wanted to take her place and attempted to enjoy herself. The way she saw it, most of the chicks at the party would be in the same place, listening to the same music, trying to fuck the same niggas ten years from now. So giving them a show of who they wished they could be was her pleasure. When the song switched to the *Terror Squad's Lean Back,* Moet went in. Marisha and Steph had gotten scooped up by a couple of fly dudes she noticed. The music was popping. Even the dudes who were trying to be cool got up and mimicked the video, and that's when she saw him.

Harry was a hood nigga by choice. He really didn't do backyard parties and bullshit like this. However, Ed was his ace and he wanted him to come. As the Terror Squad blasted from the speakers, all his boys jumped up like they were in a club and hit the dance area, but he wasn't with that shit.

He sat back and surveyed everything that was taking place. He watched his right-hand man rub up on nasty Yvette. She had a Beyoncé body but a Super head reputation.

Shaking his head, all Harry could think was, Ed better wear two rubbers if he was gonna fuck that hoe. It was amazing how many chicks at the party had been passed around. Harry knew for a fact that Yvette, China, and Renee's ass had been ran through by half of his crew. He refused to let them hoes even suck his dick. Harry wasn't the typical hood nigga; he didn't like ratchet chicks. The chicks he fucked with either already had some shit on the ball or they had goals as well as the motivation to pursue them.

If the noise level was any indication, then it appeared everyone was having a good time. Harry checked out the little set up and acknowledged it was nice for some square shit. They had an old dude fucking up the grill and plenty of non-alcoholic beverages to drink. Of course, all of the local hood rats were in attendance barely wearing any clothes. They kept cutting their eyes at him, acting like shit was sweet. If he was honest with himself, he really only had eyes for one person who was currently dancing with that whack ass nigga Superb.

Harry had been watching Moet for years. He liked the way she carried herself; she wasn't wild as hell like all these other chicks. She hung out with some cool ass chicks who had their minds on the end game. He knew Marisha was her ace in the hole and Steph was on her team also; he watched them as well. He wanted to ensure that Moet had certified ass chicks in her corner.

Every time he talked to Moet, it became even more apparent to him they were meant to be together.

He was best friends with her older cousin, Ed. Therefore, he was privy to a lot of shit about her. For instance, he knew she was abused by her mother; that she was smart, classy, didn't whore around, and shit like that. Ed loved the hell out of her, so he talked about her a lot. One thing Ed always said was he didn't like or trust that nigga Superb. Harry didn't like his punk ass either, but like Ed, he was biased. Neither of them wanted the nigga around Moet. There he was dancing real close although Moet continued to try and keep some distance between them. His bitch ass was doing some classic insecure shit; he was trying to make sure every nigga around recognized that Moet was his.

Harry simply pulled his Gucci shades back down over his eyes as he shook his head saying,

"Nigga you don't even know she already mine."

Moet had enough of dancing with Superb. She was certain he had snuck something to drink into the party because he wouldn't keep his hands off of her despite her telling him to stop.

He continued to grab her, rub on her butt, and just act a plain fool in front of her friends and family.

Some girls think that shit is cute but Moet didn't roll like that. She noticed Harry looking at her and could swear he looked pissed. Moet didn't know why this bothered her so much but it did. Every time Harry was in the same space as her and even when he wasn't, she was thinking about him.

She just didn't know what to do with what she was feeling. They shared polite conversation, he picked her up from school a couple of times when Ed couldn't make it, but he never once made a move on her. Moet was aware of what he did for a living and the nickname the streets had given him. Nevertheless, it didn't stop her from dreaming of him.

Grabbing her arm roughly, Superb snapped her attention away from Harry. He had a look of disgust on his face as he yelled over the music.

"Why the fuck you looking at that nigga? Is he the reason I can't get no pussy?"

It was like the music went on mute. Even though there weren't a lot of people paying them any attention, Moet felt the heat of the stares. Rather than have an argument and ruin her party, she attempted to just walk away. Moet was far from a punk, she was more of a silent assassin. Marisha and Steph were giving her the *we bout to fuck this nigga up look*. Moet didn't like to air her shit out in public. However, as she turned to walk away, Superb grabbed her arm again, yanking her into his chest.

Before she could blink, Superb was snatched away. It happened so fast and with so much force Moet actually stumbled backwards.

As she caught her balance, she noticed her party had completely stopped. Moet's first thought was that her girls had jumped on Superb's ass 'cause Marisha was a beast. Tables and chairs were flying as people attempted to get out of the way of the rumble that was headed their way. Moet couldn't believe her eyes as she witnessed Harry place Superb in a headlock.

Marisha and Steph ran to her side as they watched girls screaming and some of Harry's boys trying to get him to stop, but not Ed. Moet could hear Ed yelling, "Choke that nigga out Killa, choke his punk ass out." Marisha was always ready for a fight; she could be heard louder than Ed. "Yeah, fuck that bum ass nigga up." Steph was shaking her head as Moet made her way over to the altercation.

Superb was kicking his feet and struggling to remove Harry's thick arm from around his neck. He was already a light-skinned dude but right now, he looked like a straight up redneck.

She tried to avoid Superb's wild kicks as she called out to Harry, who appeared to be in a zone. "Harry, let him go. You're going to kill him, baby. I don't want you to get into any trouble, please!" She was pleading with Harry, not because she gave a fuck about what happened to Superb, he played himself. But she honestly didn't want Harry to get into any trouble.

At the same time, Harry coming to her rescue like that had her feeling a little giddy inside.

Harry looked into Moet eyes and felt an immediate calmness. He thought he was tripping, as he realized she called him baby. Harry heard the compassion in her voice then began to loosen his grip around Superb's throat. The coughing coming from Superb was loud and spit was flying everywhere.

Harry's deep voice caused the area to get quiet as he released his hold on Superb's neck. While pointing at Moet, he said,

"If you ever put your hands on that one right there again, I will fuck you up! If you ever fix your mouth to disrespect her again, I will fuck you up! And if you got a problem with what I'm saying to you, I will fuck you up!"

Moet watched as Superb weakly bobbed his head up and down, acknowledging that he understood he would get fucked up over Moet.

She watched as Harry totally released Superb and quickly got up from the ground. There was so much murmuring going on from the large crowd that Moet could hardly think. She heard a loud double clap that stole her attention away. Looking up at the balcony, she saw her Aunt Toya towering over the disrupted party. Aunt Toya was looking straight at Moet, there was a hint of disappointment in her eyes or was it understanding, but she didn't speak on it.

Instead, she yelled down to the DJ, never taking her eyes off of Moet and said,

"Crank the music back up DJ." With that, she turned and headed back into the house.

The music filled the yard again and the party-goers began to get back into the groove. Moet turned back around to see what was going on with Superb and Harry, noticing Superb was now on his feet looking dazed, but Harry was gone.

Disappointment was invading Moet's heart but she wasn't exactly sure why. Before she could dwell on it for too long, Yvette, the neighborhood skank, made it her business to put her two cents in saying,

"Harry is way too much man for you Moet."

She had a look of satisfaction on her face as she popped her gum and twirled her matted weave around her fingers.

"He needs a woman like me who knows what to do with all that." She continued.

Yvette was wearing a see through, yellow, Baby Phat cat suit. She put the S in skank and was extremely proud of it.

The laughter that came next caught Yvette by surprise. Moet couldn't help herself because Yvette was so serious about a man who didn't give two fucks about her. It was evident that her laughter was pissing Yvette off.

You could practically see fumes rising from her, but Moet didn't give a fuck. She approached her with bullshit so she would get bullshit back. Moet stepped back one step, giving Yvette a little room to wallow in her stupidity.

"Now Yvette, normally I don't even deal with bitches shit, and you know this about me. But today, I'll let you in on a little secret." She said.

Both Marisha and Steph came over to where Moet was, placing their hands on their hips. They were both ready to beat the breaks off Yvette's nasty ass. It was amusing to see Yvette tune in like she was about to learn the next winning lottery numbers. Moet smiled as she continued.

"Stop fucking niggas that don't give a fuck about you and you might find a nigga to give a fuck about you. Did you get that? 'Cause that one was free. The next one will cost you dearly." With that, Moet turned and left Yvette and the dumb ass expression on her face standing in the middle of the yard.

Marisha couldn't let it end there; she had that I will fuck you up expression on her face as she said,

"Pick your face up skank and don't get fucked up around here, 'cause we don't play that shit!" She walked away laughing with Steph on her heels about to fall out as they slapped high five.

The last of the party attendees were gone. Moet sat alone in the quiet of the Vegas night. Although her body was there, her thoughts were elsewhere.

She had known for some time she was attracted to Harry but he wasn't the typical dude. He didn't salivate over her or lose his train of thought around her. He was sure of himself and very intelligent. She even loved having superficial conversations with him. Smiling to herself, Moet decided she needed to explore this attraction before she went off to college. Making herself comfortable, she felt her eyelids get heavy, it had been a long and exciting day.

She never noticed The Watcher lurking in the shadows, spying on her every move.

*****

Cruising the strip, Harry had the music low. He was deep in thought but still on guard. At 24-years-old, he was already a street legend with a deadly reputation. He was the illegitimate son of Henry *The Butcher* Blake, one of the wealthiest men in Vegas who had lucrative business dealings in Vegas both legitimate and underground. His mother, Markita, was a beautiful woman with looks that could put almost any man in a trance. She was a blackjack dealer in one of his father's casinos and eventually found her way into his bed. Harry knew all about the love affair between his parents. It was legendary in Vegas; some people saw his mother as the ghetto girl who hit the jackpot. Some say it was a shame the way his father stepped out on his family. Regardless of what individuals on the outside saw, what they didn't know was his parents were very much in love.

His father raised him in the underworld and gave him every opportunity to reign supreme in that environment. He had two older half-brothers, Henry, Jr. and Hector, who were raised to run the legitimate casino businesses. Henry, Jr. ran The Lime Light and Hector ran The Straight Shooter. They knew who Harry was and what he did for the family. Mostly, they stayed out of his way. His father always claimed him; he just never introduced him to his other world.

Harry and his mother were always okay with this arrangement because in the underworld, he was the son of The Butcher. It just so happens, that Harry was a chip off the old block. The streets called him Killa which is exactly what he did. The money laundering end of the family business always had someone who needed to be dealt with or collected from and that's where Harry came in.

The shattering of his back window caused Harry to swerve but maintain control of his vehicle. Seeing a slight shadow in his rearview, he was determined to give them exactly what they were looking for.

At the corner of East St. Louis and South Main St. near the welcome to Las Vegas sign, he screeched his tires to a halt and quickly placed his car in park.

Before anyone could regain their senses, Harry was out of the passenger door blasting both of his Walther PPK's at his would be executioners. The first bullet splattered the brains of the driver over the windshield.

The passenger, who quickly jumped from the car, was more concerned about the brain matter on him than the deadly assassin who was coming his way. The first bullet hit him in the shoulder. Harry wanted to get his attention.

The man jerked back from the impact of the bullet. Quickly regaining his footing, he started firing his weapon over the car in Harry's direction. Stealthy, Harry moved to the opposite side of his original position. His next shot took the man off his feet and landed him on the nearby median. Harry stood over a moaning, bloody mass of shit. He looked down into the man's face, trying to recognize him but he didn't. As he turned to walk away, Harry fired straight down into his face, thinking and no one else will recognize him either.

Thirty minutes later, he pulled his bullet riddled car into the private garage at The Lime Light Casino where he had a two bedroom bungalow suite. He needed to meet with his team and try to figure out who needed to be killed first. Harry was pissed that someone had the balls to come for him. Nevertheless, he realized there was always one punk willing to jump up to get beat down. He was just the one to put the lead to that ass. When he entered the hotel, he always used the private elevator, not wanting to draw attention to himself. His father's family didn't like that he got the same perks as a Blake, but they could suck his dick because he was a Blake.

As he entered his suite, his main goal was to wash the day off. Thoughts of a satisfying hot shower guided him toward the bathroom. The water cascaded down his muscular back.

His six foot length was dwarfed in the huge Jacuzzi shower. The massive jets sprayed him from several directions while he washed the day away and thought about Moet. The steam emitted a heavy fog in the spacious bathroom; Moet's beautiful frame filled his brain. To him, she was the strongest woman he knew due to her enduring the abuse she had encountered at an early age and being fatherless.

Ed told him everything about her. Truthfully, that's when Harry realized he wanted to be the one to protect her always. Harry was even more convinced it was time to bring her into his world. He was aware that she had plans to attend college and he would support her aspirations to the fullest. However, he needed her in his life. He waited until she was legal and had completed high school. This was a promise he made to Ed, but now was the time and he didn't care who didn't like it.

*****

The smack across the face sent 15-year-old Moet flying across the room. Bruce started unzipping his pants as he walked across the room. He looked as if he was foaming at the mouth as he said,

"Every pussy in this house belongs to me bitch. I pay the mortgage in this bitch and all the fucking bills. When I want my dick sucked, all I want you to do is drop to ya knees."

Moet refused to cry in front of anybody, but she also wasn't going to sit there and let her mother's nasty ass boyfriend take something from her he had no right to.

She couldn't imagine where her mother was; she never left men around when she wasn't home. Once again, she felt her mother had let her down.

Lecretia was jealous of her well-stacked daughter. At 15-years-old, Moet Rollins was absolutely stunning. She stood 5'7", 145 lbs. with beautiful, bronze skin and the brains to match.

She had amazing manners and poise; most people mistook her for a model. Lecretia was a knockout herself. Sadly, she viewed Moet's beauty as a threat rather than being proud of her daughter. She felt as though Moet was her competition. Consequently, she blamed Moet for everything that she felt was fucked up in her life.

Bruce was in a zoned out as he stood in front of Moet with his dick hanging out of his pants. He wasn't trying to hear any of Moet's pleas. I've waited a year for this pussy, paid plenty of money for this pussy, this pussy is mine, he thought.

He had never seen anything more beautiful than Moet and was salivating at the thought of tasting her. The disgusted look on Moet's face didn't deter him not one bit. Bruce was arrogant and couldn't imagine why a woman wouldn't want to be with him; he was handsome, fit, and had deep pockets.

Hell, that's how he scooped up her momma in the first place; she wasn't even the one he was checking for; he always wanted Moet. Bruce recognized to get to the daughter, sometimes you had to go through the momma which is exactly what he did.

He ran his game on Lecretia already sensing she was a bitch about her paper. He made Lecretia feel like she was the queen she thought she was. He dicked her down properly, kept her pockets fat, and her bills paid. Over the year, he could sense the hate Lecretia had for her daughter. Hence, he played on that.

He told Lecretia shit like Moet wasn't making no money out there fucking for free; and that she might as well make some money off of her since she had been providing the lap of luxury for her ass all her life. Bruce even went as far as to say Moet owed her. When he proposed that he be the one to break Moet in just to make sure the shit was done right, he knew he had Lecretia sprung. Eventually, he gave Lecretia's money hungry ass $30,000 to take Moet's virginity.

Bruce was the one who talked Lecretia out of saving for Moet's college tuition. Instead, he told her to take a vacation and go on a shopping spree. He knew Moet was counting on her mother paying for college in four years because that's all she talked about. Bruce planned to use this as a chip to lure her to his bed.

Moet perceived what was going on in Bruce's mind as he stood in front of her with his dick in his hand stroking it back and forth. She had never seen a dick in person but she wasn't stupid. It wasn't that Moet wasn't interested in boys; it's just that they always only seemed to want to have sex.

She grew up seeing her mother use sex as a way to get things and Moet wanted no part of it. Her original plan was to go to college, fall in love, begin a career, get married, and start a family. Moet felt the best way to accomplish that goal was to keep her legs closed. She spent a lot of time at her Aunt Toya's house where her dreams were fostered. During these visits, she made plans for her future along with her home girl, Marisha, who had the same dreams.

Those dreams were shattered when her mother unceremoniously told her she had spent all of her college savings. This shattered Moet's spirit until her mother told her Bruce may have a plan on how to get the tuition paid. Moet's eyes turned black as it now dawned on her what plan Bruce had. Her soul needed to know if her mother knew about it. Therefore, she asked with a quiver in her voice,

"Does my mother know what you're trying to do to me, Bruce?"

Licking his lips as he stroked his dick, Bruce was nodding his head up and down.

"You're paid for; I'm gonna break that sweet pussy in then I'm gonna make some money off of your fine ass. Yo momma can't save you; she don't even like your ass. If you want me to put aside any money for college, you better bend that sweet ass over." Bruce looked satisfied with himself like he had solved some great puzzle.

Something died in Moet right then. It was always extremely difficult for her to understand why her mother didn't like her. They never had a genuine mother-daughter connection. But to sell her daughter to the highest bidder was a new low, even for her. She couldn't believe her mother would take her dislike this far. Moet didn't know who her father was and her mother refused to tell her.

Anytime Moet asked about him, she got cursed out. Moet felt sick to her stomach and disgusted by the spectacle in front of her. But her favorite cousin, Ed, had told her just how to deal with nasty boys the last time she visited her Aunt Toya. He said,

"Let they nasty ass get close and then grab hold of their dick with a vice grip that won't stop and try to break that motherfucker." He burst out laughing after he said it.

Right now, it was exactly what she needed for her survival. The closer Bruce got with his man meat sticking out like an arrow, the more frightened she became. Moet was thinking what if it doesn't work and he grabs me or beats me? Deciding she would rather go out fighting than just lie down and take the abuse, she readied herself. She was perspiring and her nerves were on end.

Bruce couldn't see anything pass Moet's beauty. The plans he had for her were making the tip of his dick throb. He had convinced himself she wanted him just as much as he wanted her.

For that reason, the closer he got, his mind was swirling with anticipation of being able to suck on some virgin pussy. The smile on his face would have lit up the room if the situation wasn't so grave.

He had never had a virgin before. As he stroked his dick, he recalled how he was tricked the first time he was supposed to get some virgin pussy. His very first girlfriend was touched by someone before he dug in her. That's probably where this compulsion for young girls started. Now it was his turn. As he reached out to touch Moet's face, he was happy to see her reaching for his dick. Pre-cum was seeping out; he felt himself overcome with anticipation.

Just as sure as the excitement came, the pain took over. At first, he didn't understand what was happening. He thought maybe she just didn't know what she was doing, but it became obvious after a scream that started from his toes finally made it pass his vocal cords. Moet also screamed and damn near pulled his dick out of socket. Bruce immediately fell to his knees and tried to ease the pain he was in. Before he could even comfort himself a little, Moet grabbed the baseball bat from the corner of her room and whacked him twice in the head.

Moet didn't wait around to see if she had killed Bruce. She grabbed her cell phone and ran out of the house. The tears flowing down her cheeks were nothing compared to how bad she was shaking. In that instant, she was more pissed than scared.

Rather than calling the police right away, she called her cousin, Ed, who was yelling into the phone that he was gonna skin folks alive. He told her to run to the neighbor's house and call the police.

The patio door closing saved Moet from her nightmare. She sat up quickly and looked around to ensure she wasn't still in that horrible place and time; she was continually plagued by the nightmares. A light sweat had formed around her forehead and she could feel the headache forming that she normally had after these dreams. It wasn't Bruce who haunted her, it was Lecretia. She couldn't even call her mother anymore. Her family tried to help her as much as they could but Ed was always her hero.

When he arrived on the scene the night of the attack with Aunt Toya, the ambulance was just pulling Bruce out of the house on a stretcher. They stopped to allow the police to handcuff him to the gurney. He was screaming that he wanted Moet arrested for assault and battery. Ed put his arms around Moet and said,

"He hasn't seen assault and battery yet lil cuzzo, believe that. His days are numbered."

The police sent Moet home with her aunt and put an all-points bulletin out for her mother. That was three years ago; she had been with Aunt Toya and Ed ever since.

Ed made his way toward Moet. The slight breeze in the Vegas air was rare, but it felt good just the same. He watched her from the door for a while.

He could see her tossing and turning and immediately knew she was reliving her attack and the pain she felt by her mother's betrayal. Ed hated his Aunt Lecretia. She disgusted him.

He was raised by a wonderful and loving mother. As a result, he never understood why her sister could be such an unloving person. Ed couldn't understand how she could hate her own daughter so much. The justice system never caught up with his aunt. For three years, she had eluded them. The law stopped actively searching for her years ago although there is still an active warrant in the books. Ed never stopped looking for her. Bruce was another story.

Despite how much his mother tried, she couldn't keep Ed out of the streets. He was just like his father, E Dog, who ran one of the toughest street crews in Vegas. That's actually how he originally met Harry. Ed's father worked for Harry's father, so the boys had been around each other since the sandbox. E Dog was killed in a raid by the police five years ago. Ed started spending more and more time with The Butcher and Harry. He was being trained to fill his father's shoes. Initially, Toya was totally against it, but she could see the determination in her son's eyes. Hence, she decided to support him like she supported his father and prayed for the best.

When he was out with his crew, part of his mind was always on his Aunt Lecretia and the death he was destined to deal out to her. Eventually, he let his best friend, Harry, in on that part of Moet's life. Ed wasn't stupid; he knew Harry was feeling Moet.

They had known each other a long time. Harry was the best dude he knew, loyal, deadly, and caked up.

He would take care of Moet and deliver death to anyone who fucked with her. Ed knew his mom wanted Moet to finish school and go to college. She didn't get that from him since he stayed in the street, so he was determined to ensure that Moet had the opportunity. Harry understood that and promised he wouldn't stand in the way of it.

Ed smiled as he remembered how Harry jumped on Superb's weak ass today. Thinking to himself, bitch ass nigga think he gonna run through my lil cuzzo, fuck outta here. This wasn't the first time Harry had laid hands on someone over Moet.

A year ago, they caught up with Bruce as he exited a local nightspot with two young girls on his arms. Ed noticed him first and pointed him out to Harry who immediately forgot his desire to have a drink. They got back in their Beamer and followed closely behind. They watched as Bruce pulled into a dusty, local motel and ushered the two young girls into a room. Ed had fire brewing in his eyes as he said,

"This nigga still trying to fuck little girls. I'm 'bout to end him Killa. He got to go." There was a scowl on his face that equated to death to whomever it was directed at.

Harry was quiet, he was thinking about the pain and hurt this nigga had brought to his Moet. That was all he needed as he stepped from the car and headed toward the motel.

The night sky shielded them and the seclusion of the motel was its partner in crime. Harry kicked the door open with his size 13 Timberlands, startling Bruce who had his dick in one girl's mouth while he played with the other girl's big ass titties.

Ed moved in quickly and closed what was left of the door with his pistols pointed at both girls. Bruce recognized him immediately and had the nerve to jump bad with four pistols in the room. He looked at Ed and said,

"I know your bitch ass is not still pissed over that little slut. I didn't even fuck her man."

It was like he didn't realize those were his last moments on earth as he kept running his trap.

"Her grimy ass momma sold her to me, so I wasn't taking nothing that wasn't rightfully mine anyway nigga."

Before he could get another word out, Harry bust him in the mouth with his Sig Sauer, opening up a huge gash in his lip. Bruce's mouth swelled up to the size of a tennis ball, stopping all talking.

Harry gave Ed a look. Ed looked at the girls and said,

"Under any other circumstance, I would be telling you to stop going to hotels with strange perverts. Unfortunately, you ladies won't have the opportunity to put that advice into practice."

One of the girls started to scream. Consequently, she was the first to catch a bullet right between her eyes. The other girl simply stared at Ed, not crying or even looking fearful. She kind of looked relieved. Ed shot her without another thought then turned back to Bruce who was bleeding all over the nasty, musty carpet.

He pointed his weapon at him and said, "Fucking with my family cost you your life."

With that, he fired two bullets, center mass chest and forehead. Harry gave him a strong head nod then they backed out of the room like nothing ever happened.

Ed took a seat next to Moet and immediately wrapped his large arms around her shoulder. To him, Moet represented strength. People slept on her because she didn't do the typical hood rat shit. He was happy she had friends like Marisha and Steph because they were no nonsense and would throw hands with Moet if needed.

As she lay in his arms, he made the decision that it was time for Harry to step in, train her, and love her.

Still lurking in the shadows, The Watcher became visibly upset at the affection Ed showed Moet. The deep seeded desire to disrupt this happy family was forming, causing the lurker to get excited as the observation continued.

*****

A week after the graduation party, Moet rushed around the house getting things ready to go to UNLV for a tour and orientation with her girls.

Ed was coming to pick her up; if she wasn't ready, she would never hear the end of it. She made sure she had her ID, birth certificate, social security card, and extra money. Smiling to herself, she felt completely prepared for the day. Marisha and Steph were going to meet her on campus. The three of them together on the UNLV campus, college life just wasn't ready for that. Just thinking about it gave Moet butterflies. She stopped and picked up a picture from her dresser of her and Marisha sitting on the hood of Ed's green Cutlass Supreme. They had to be about 13-years-old in that picture. No one but the two of them really knew and understood the abusive hell they were privately going through. They shared their story with each other which strengthened them.

Aunt Toya was in the kitchen preparing dinner when Moet entered. She just stood in the doorway and stared at her aunt as she sung, *Happy Feelings,* by her favorite group, Maze and Frankie Beverly. It made Moet feel good to know her aunt was happy. Aunt Toya had been to her what she needed all her life.

She apologized for the way Lecretia was, but Moet told her not to do that. The way Lecretia acted was not Aunt Toya's fault. As a child, Moet could recall many a day where her aunt had come and rescued her from Lecretia's neglectful ass. Now that she was an adult herself, she still couldn't fathom what made Lecretia act the way she did. Moet made a promise to herself to be the best wife and mother she could be after she secured her future with a good career.

Clearing her throat, she alerted her Aunt Toya that she was in the room. Otherwise, she would swear you were trying to scare her to death. Stirring something on the stove that smelled marvelous, she turned toward Moet and smiled, saying,

"Ms. Lady, I knew you were standing there, don't be acting like I'm old." She winked at Moet and kept stirring her food as she continued.

"I'm very proud of you Moet. I really need you to understand that." The bobbing up and down of her head indicated to Toya that Moet understood what she was saying.

The horn beeping outside notified her that Ed's impatient ass was on time as usual. Toya wiped her hand on her apron and headed out the kitchen fussing.

"I know this boy not in my yard blowing no damn horn like he crazy."

Moet followed behind her laughing because she knew the antics were about to begin. Ed and his mother had the best relationship. They were always picking with each other but the affection and love they had for one another was clearly evident. Seeing them in action always made Moet feel better about her jacked up situation–a mother who doesn't love you and not knowing who your father is.

When they opened the door and walked into the driveway, each woman was dumbfounded by what they saw. With a huge, red bow around it there was a 2004 Mercedes Benz Roadster Convertible. It was the cutest thing Moet had ever seen in her life. She ran like a track star and jumped into her cousin's arms, hugging and kissing him from cheek to cheek, yelling,

"Oh my god Ed, thank you; thank you; thank you!"

Even Toya forgot she was about to come out and do her normal clowning and fuss her son out. She too was excited at the present her son had blessed his cousin with.

Ed put Moet down, grinning from ear-to-ear. He was happy that she liked the car. She deserved some happiness in her life. He wondered how she would feel after she found out he wasn't the one who bought it for her.

Reaching into his back pocket, he handed her a large envelope. Moet stared at the envelope, shaking her head back and forth. She wouldn't take it saying, "Ed, you're always looking out for me and I'm so grateful but that's enough. I don't need anything else. My car is wonderful." The laughter coming from Ed stopped her in the middle of her sermon. Moet had a perplexed expression on her face as she hit Ed in his chest and laughed with him. They both watched as Toya took a seat in the car and inspected the interior. During that time, Ed took the opportunity to say,

"Moet open the envelope, everything will be explained. I have to run and will talk to you later."

Before she could make a fuss, Ed kissed her on the cheek, jumped back in his car, and peeled off.

*****

After they completed orientation, Moet, Marisha, and Steph sat on a bench in the UNLV courtyard. The plush greenery was very inviting and the men walking by added to the scenery. Steph was shaking her head as she watched all the walking sex pass her and her girls. Throwing her hands in the air, she yelled out,

"I'm gonna get myself in trouble at this school, I can just feel it."

The girls were laughing and joking and expressing their excitement about being grown. They always enjoyed themselves when they were together. Their personalities meshed well. Steph was quiet but a scrapper. She didn't take no shit, but she didn't start none either.

She was Marisha's neighbor. They had been close friends for years before Moet started coming to the neighborhood. Marisha was the loud one who would give you the *I will fuck you up look in a minute*. She was always looking for a fight, mainly because she had to fight all her life.

Her mother was abused and she took the brunt of beatings herself until she started fighting back. The similar backgrounds bonded Marisha and Moet together but their love for each other made them all go so hard for each other. Moet was the watcher of the crew. She wasn't one to take any shit. Therefore, you would never see her coming if she was ready to let loose. Together these three girls made a pact to stay fly and focused. They refused to be ran through like the girls they saw everyday so they encouraged each other. Sitting on the bench today and laughing with each other was just a small fulfillment of their promise to one another.

When Marisha announced she had a confession to make, both of her girls gave her a look that said spill the beans. Being her normal, dramatic self, Marisha pushed her braids to the side and looked both of her girls in the eye as she said,

"I have a crush on Ed."

Both Moet and Steph fell out laughing. The laughter was so loud it caught the attention of people passing by. The girls were just having way too much fun. Marisha got up with her hands on her hips and yelled through her own laughter,

"Why are y'all heffa's laughing? I'm gonna make Ed my man. I ain't thinking about these UNLV niggas, I want Ed."

Moet settled down, waving her hand in the air, attempting to regain her composure. However, the pout Marisha was wearing made Moet topple over again as she said,

"I'm just messing with you Marisha. I know you're serious. My cousin is a good dude, and he couldn't do any better than you. We were just laughing because you acting like we didn't already know that shit."

Because the shit was funny, they all burst out laughing again. They were the best of friends and shared everything with each other.

Looking through her purse, Moet found the white envelope Ed had given her, remembering he said it would explain everything, she opened it up. The brightness of her eyes told her girls something was up, so Steph asked,

"What is it Mo?"

Moet was still flipping through all the hundred dollar bills that were neatly placed in the envelope. She wasn't new to money. Ed gave her money all the time, but this was the most money she had ever held in her hands. She looked at her girls and said,

"Ed gave me this envelope this morning when he dropped off the car and told me to open it, it would explain everything. I just hadn't done it yet. My gosh, there has to be like $5,000 in here."

All the girls screamed in unison. Moet opened the note inside the envelope and started reading it aloud.

Mo,

If you're reading this, that means Ed has delivered my gift to you. I hope you like it. I picked it out with you in mind. Take the money in this envelope and you and your girls do what you do, but meet me at Joel Robuchon in The Lime Light at 8 p.m.

Harry

P.S. It's our time.

Once again, the screaming coming from the trio drew attention as each girl re-read the note out loud. Internally, Moet was smiling as she stared off in space. She wanted so much to explore her feelings for Harry, but she wanted him to meet the adult Moet. For that reason, she jumped up from the bench and told her girls,

"Let's go ladies. We have a lot of work to do. Marisha, leave your car here and you guys ride with me. We 'bout to get right."

*****

Moet stepped into The Lime Light with her girls looking like new money. She was in a little black Chanel dress that hugged her waist just right and a pair of five inch Gucci heels that made her legs look like a runway models. The day at the spa and a total makeover from head-to-toe had her feeling and looking like a million bucks. Heads were turning in the large Casino lobby. More than one man stopped to try and get their attention. Women were giving them that I hate you bitches stare, which made Moet giggle on the inside.

It meant the total makeover not only was a success but was visibly noticeable. Entering the restaurant, she was taken aback by the fancy décor and large amount of people looking like they could buy the hotel.

Checking her girls out, she had to admit they were bad. Steph was taller than Moet, at least 5'10" with legs that seemed to go on forever. Her body appeared to be sculpted and the burnt orange Dolce & Gabbana she was wearing was everything.

Marisha never stepped out in anything lower than seven inches. Thanks to Harry, she was finally able to get those Jimmy Choo's she had been eyeing for months. She was only 5'5" but always appeared to be taller. Her body was accentuated by the latest Marc Jacob one piece pantsuit. The red color accentuated her highlights and gave her all the attention she could handle, both wanted and unwanted. The ladies were ushered to a reserved private room. When they strolled through the door, all conversation came to a halt.

Harry couldn't believe what he was seeing. This could not be Moet. It looked like her but a grown and sexy version of her. He didn't mean to stare but the way that dress was hugging her thickness was making the monster in his Gucci slacks very uncomfortable. All of the girls were on point. But Moet, she was exquisite. Overnight she had transformed into a sexy ass, grown woman, or was she always this woman and he just refused to see it.

Dupree and Ed were damn near drooling at the sight of Marisha and Steph. Ed had been keeping his eye on Marisha but never made a move; she was Moet's girl and he didn't want to step to her unless he was really ready to do something. He also knew that Marisha experienced a lot of the same shit Moet went through and it broke a nigga's heart to know that. Looking at her right now though, Ed was about to rethink this hands off doctrine he had declared, thinking to himself, she's ready. Ed broke the silence by saying,

"Damn y'all asses is phat to death."

All of the nervous energy everyone was experiencing evaporated at that moment. Laughter could be heard throughout the elegant and spacious room. Standing behind a chair, Ed motioned for Marisha to come forward. She made sure to put on her extra sexy walk and stifle the butterflies she was encountering.

Dupree made space next to him for Steph. He was a real quiet dude, most said he had a deadly silence. But no one could deny how handsome he was. At 5'11" with a rock hard body and mocha skin tone, he never had a problem getting women. He just didn't have the patience for foolishness. Dupree got that from his dad.

His dad always told him, to never settle for a woman who was only bringing pussy to the table. He watched Steph from the background for years as she developed into the beautiful woman he was currently observing. He knew she wasn't about the hood shit and actually had a head on her shoulders.

Pulling out a chair for her, he never diverted his eyes off of her flawless skin thinking, it might be time to see what Steph is talking about.

Harry had prearranged a five course dinner from the Cabernet Filet Mignon menu. He wanted to show everyone a good time and introduce them to some wonderful cuisine. If there was one perk to living in The Lime Light, it was the menu choices in the four, world star restaurants.

The conversation was light and festive as the first course was placed on the table by the immaculately dressed waiter. The smell of the Maryland Crab Cakes served with a Green Onion Sauce was to die for.

All conversation ceased, the only thing that could be heard were the sweet sounds of Baby face playing over the restaurant speakers and forks clinking against fine china. By the time they got to the main course, there wasn't a dissatisfied face in the room. The waiters blessed the table with Cabernet Filet Mignon, a Perfect Baked Potato, and Asparagus Parmigiano. Moet was in absolute heaven. As a result, she said,

"This is wonderful Harry, it really is."

She thanked him a couple more times for the car and the makeover as well. He was staring at her as she sat across the table.

"Anything you need, I got you. I'm glad you like the car."

He admired her blushing face. Shit, he liked everything about Moet, and he was man enough to admit it to himself.

The light R&B music breezing through the restaurant had him feeling good; he didn't want the night to end. Getting the attention of his boys, he said,

"Hey fellas y'all up for trying your hand on the tables?"

Harry already knew Ed was down to toss some bread on the table, but Dupree was another story. He was a more laid-back dude with a deadly grip. On the contrary, it appeared he was down for some action tonight, or was it Steph who was bringing it out of him. The thought made Harry smile; he loved to see his team be able to enjoy themselves. Normally, they were all business. Everyone got up from the table to make their way out of the private section with nothing but having a good time on their minds.

The desire to be held by Harry overtook her body. It was a bold move but she was determined to make it. Moving around the table to meet him as he was advancing in her direction, Moet fell into his arms. It was the first time she had ever been held by him. It was like the melting of cotton candy after it enters your mouth; she literally sank into his body. He pulled her into his chest kissing her on her forehead. The Armani Code sent chills down her spine and the tingling in her womanhood almost made her lose her balance but Harry had her.

Harry held her tightly and whispered in her ear,

"It's our time."

Holding her close, he kissed her forehead again. Moet felt safe in his embrace; it was no longer necessary to question what she was feeling.

There was a loud crash coming from the main dining room area. Everyone assumed it was a waiter dropping someone's meal until a scream reverberated from the ceiling. Harry released Moet and grabbed his twin Sig Sauer's from his back, made eye contact with Ed then made his way toward the entrance.

His team was by his side, all packing and ready to make some noise. Gunfire could be heard; the team knew what time it was. Harry gave Moet a head nod to get down, but she needed to get to her girls. She removed her stilettos and headed in their direction. Before she could make it from her side of the table to her girls, a scream that almost caused Moet's eardrums to burst could be heard coming from Steph. Moet ran over to her and was met by Dupree with pistol in hand and a look of hatred on his face. What they saw when they made it to Steph's side caused Moet to fall to her knees. Steph joined Moet on the restaurant floor as they watched the life escape from their best friend's eyes. Marisha was on the floor with a hole the size of a quarter between her eyes. She looked like she was sleeping, but the blood spilling from her forehead told a different story.

Time appeared to stand still. Moet didn't know how long she stayed on the floor looking into her best friend's lovely face. But the next thing she knew, Harry was scooping her from the floor and out the only exit while simultaneously firing in the direction of the intruders.

Moet remained in a fog; she couldn't believe she had loss the closest thing to a sister she would ever have. Before her mind could dwell on it further, Harry pushed her to the restaurant floor just as a shot flew pass her and landed in a waitress's head who was walking right behind her.

The restaurant was a war zone. Retaliation by Harry, Ed, and Dupree was swift and certain. Patrons were hiding behind tables. Unfortunately, a number of them had fallen victim to gunfire.

Harry grabbed Moet from the floor and put her behind the bar as he continued to fire in the direction of the heat. Moet frantically peaked around the bar and tried to find Steph through the smoke and destruction; she couldn't lose her too. There was so much chaos inside the restaurant that it was now spilling onto the casino floor. It became a challenge to know what direction the bullets were coming from.

Moet saw the body of one of the niggas responsible for ending the life of her best friend sprawled out on the restaurant floor. He was dead but it was not enough for her. Without thinking, she left from behind the bar and picked up the semi-automatic weapon that was near his body. She was in a state of consciousness so intense the chaos around her didn't exist.

Moet had never shot a gun before. However, she had held a gun that Ed left on his bed once, so she didn't feel totally uncomfortable. The last time she felt this out of control, she had just bashed Lecretia's boyfriend's head in. All she wanted to see or know right now was death. She now recognized that if pushed, there was a fire in her that would be hard to extinguish. Her body and mind ached so badly. She couldn't stop the tears from cascading down her face as she pulled the trigger repeatedly, unloading into the already dead body. Nonetheless, the screams coming from her soul didn't quench her need for revenge. Moet turned, aiming the gun toward the room as her eyes searched for Steph and a way out.

A loud whistle could be heard over all the screaming. Moet wasn't thinking clearly but something told her it was Harry calling for her. Glass and bodies were everywhere. She aimed her weapon but before she could make a move, she was grabbed and pulled so violently she was certain something had cracked. Her scream vibrated off the walls, but the gunfire that ensued was its deadly competition. Harry and Ed both emptied their clips into her would be assailant. Just as quickly, Harry was by Moet's side.

He could see the pain she was in but realized it wasn't just about being jacked up by the dead nigga. It was a consequence of losing her girl. He saw her bust a gun into the dead dude and hoped that's what she needed to begin to deal with the situation. Not everyone could handle death.

If he could spare her, he would. Right now, he had to get her the hell out of The Lime Light. Bending down to pick Moet up, Harry wrapped his strong arms around her. All the while, keeping his eye on the front door of the restaurant. Glancing around, it was pure madness.

Dupree had Steph with him, but when his eyes made their way to Ed, he could see him on one knee in front of Marisha. Harry's body stiffened, he realized there was no way to spare Moet from the pain of witnessing her cousin going through his emotions. Moet was holding firmly onto Harry's neck, she felt him tense up. She said,

"Let me down baby, I need to see Marisha again."

Reluctantly, Harry did as she asked. Then again, he knew they needed to leave. Vegas Metro was assuredly en route. Furthermore, his brother, Henry, Jr., would be assuredly get his ass whooped if he came in there with some bullshit. For that reason, it was time to bounce.

Moet and Steph both said their goodbyes to Marisha. There were tears of regret cascading down Moet's face. Ed comforted her as he whispered in her ear, "Baby girl, I'm so sorry, but we got to bounce before we all end up in jail." Moet gave him a hard nod, indicating she understood. Standing up, she and Steph followed as they were led out of the restaurant, stepping over a number of bodies on their way out the door. Moet's insides tightened as she stepped over the last body, she was leaving her friend in this restaurant on the floor. Another thing she was leaving was her innocence.

Her heart hurt more than she could explain to anyone. For that, someone had to pay.

*****

A week later, Moet sat up screaming into the darkness. She was sweating profusely and shaking. The vision of Marisha laying in her casket continued to invade her dreams. The way her heartbeat was racing made Moet place her hand on her chest to still her aching heart. A light touch on her leg startled her but comforted her at the same time. She turned slightly to see Harry sitting up on his elbows, staring with an expression of concern. The only way she had gotten through this week was due to the care and concern Harry had shown her.

Since the night of the attack, she had been with him. Initially, her Aunt Toya was not happy about it, but Harry explained how he felt about Moet. And he would give his life before he allowed anything to happen to her.

Toya told Moet she had seen that look before from a man and could only describe it as love. She entrusted her niece to Harry. In turn, he agreed to help heal her heart. Moet was still shaking as Harry pulled her into his arms and wrapped her in his warmth. Moet melted into his embrace then the floodgates opened up. She sobbed for Marisha and the dreams she would never fulfill. Moet mourned her friend as Harry held her and stroked her hair. There were no words spoken, just comfort and understanding.

Moet fell asleep in his arms. He held her as she went through her emotions over losing her home girl. Harry never realized he embodied this level of emotion. He spent so much time being a cold-hearted nigga he didn't believe love was even in the cards for him. Without a doubt, as he watched her breathe in and out, he comprehended Moet was what his heart desired. She represented the good in him; he needed her to bring balance into his world.

Getting up from the bed without waking her, Harry took a shower and got dressed. He had a meeting set up with his team. There had already been two attempts on his life; there would not be a third.

He met with his father and was not surprised that The Butcher was ready to come out of retirement and make the streets bleed once again. Harry assured him he would take care of it. He was further amazed that even his brothers, Henry and Hector, were on board. Harry didn't think they had a gangsta bone in their bodies. Nonetheless, they both were at the meeting with their dad, pledging their support. His father had ears on the street. He informed Harry that one of the assassins survived the gunfight at The Lime Light and was in the Summerlin Medical Center. Harry promised on everything he wasn't making it out of there alive, but he needed to find out who hired him first.

*****

Sitting up in his hospital bed after a week of unconsciousness, Bernard Bottom was looking around the room for a way out. He knew shit was going to get real once niggas realized he was still alive.

With a shattered shoulder and a concussion, he was no worse for the wear, but fucking up a job like the hit on Harry and his team was sure to end his life one way or another.

In addition, Vegas Metro was stationed outside his door waiting for him to be cleared for release so they could hall his ass off to jail. Moving slowly, he began to put his clothes on as his mind replayed the tragic event.

He watched his brother, Dante, catch a bullet. What he wasn't prepared for was to watch some bitch dump bullets into his body. And when his brother, Andreas, snatched her little ass up, Harry and Ed unloaded bullets into him. Dupree had Brandon pinned down at the time, but he didn't miss a thing. The pain of seeing his brothers gunned down was more than he could take. He made a quick move for the door but was cut down by Dupree before he made it. The bullet shattered his shoulder but falling through the glass table knocked him unconscious.

The Bottom Brothers didn't grow up in Vegas; they were transplants from Oakland. They were five of the deadliest men in Vegas; Andreas, Bernard, Corey, Dante, and Eric. In their old neighborhood, they were known as the alphabet boys because their first names began with the first five letters of the alphabet.

In opposition, they were far from the Feds, they were killers for hire. Completely dressed, Brandon peaked outside of his hospital room, noticing the shift change had begun.

Although he had been unconscious for a week, he had faked the last couple of days so he could get an understanding of his surroundings and plan his escape. One thing he observed was there was a thirty minute period where he was not guarded daily. Peeking out the door now, he only had twenty minutes left to make his escape.

Brandon needed to make this right. His plan was to contact Corey and Eric and finish the job they were hired for. Not only was their reputation on the line, but they had to deal with the wrath of their mother due to Andreas and Dante's death. He feared that more than the death that would come at the hands of their employer. Deciding the stairs would be the best escape route, he headed that way just as he heard the chime from the elevator.

From the window of the staircase, he took a look to see who was getting off the elevator and noticed Harry and Ed with their pistols drawn. Quickly descending the stairs, he was determined not to die today.

*****

It had been three weeks since the worst day of her life. During that time, she had made some internal decisions. Her heart was still heavy, but her tears had dried up. In fact, she didn't think she had any more.

What she wanted more than anything was to cause pain to the people responsible for her loss. Sitting in the den which was elegant and stylish and decorated in a hue of burnt orange and brown, Moet waited for Harry and Ed to return. She didn't need them on board to put her plan into effect. She just needed to holla at Steph. The 60 inch television mounted to the wall was on but there was no sound. She had never been more determined about anything in her life.

Walking over to the bar and fixing herself a club soda, Moet thought to herself, I am so tired of people thinking I'm something to play with. It's time they find out the real.

She was so deep in thought, she didn't hear him enter, but she could smell the Armani as he got closer. Moet decided to play it off like she didn't know he was there until Harry wrapped his arms around her waist and kissed her hair. She took a sharp breath; the feeling was amazing. Every time Harry wrapped her in his arms, she felt love. She turned to face him and took his tongue in her mouth. They had yet to take that final step. Yet, Moet felt that if she wanted to give herself to anyone, Harry would be the man. The bulge in his pants was pressed against her thigh. The mere size of it was intimidating, but the sensations building in her body were making her brave and bold. Grabbing Harry's hand, Moet led him to the huge bedroom suite. She was unsure of what to do but not confused about why she was there.

Harry could feel her apprehension and excitement all bundled up together. He loved the innocence Moet possessed and her trust in him. He wanted her to know what real love felt like. Once they made it to the king sized bed, he lay her on top of the plush, brown comforter and began to kiss her from head-to-toe, paying special attention to the sensitive parts of her body. Removing clothes as they progressed, he watched her melt under his touch. His own breathing was labored. He was finally about to possess the one woman that consumed him. The moaning coming from Moet was the sexiest thing Harry had ever heard. It was like a song that brings back good memories every time you hear it. Tracing his tongue over her nipples, he could feel her heart racing.

Placing both of her legs on his shoulders, his intention was to take her to a place she never even imagined. Her smell was intoxicating and her juices sweet. Moet was squirming so much Harry had to hold on as he continued to taste every inch of her insides. There was a loud thunderous scream that came from the tip of her toes and made it to her vocal cords right before the damn broke; Harry was invited to swim in her ocean. Moet was shaking uncontrollably as well as uttering a succession of whimpering. Harry wanted to feel her tightness but he didn't want to hurt her. He began rubbing his girth up and down over her clit; he could feel her breathing begin to match his own. Placing only the head in, the tightness sent shivers through his body.

It was his plan to take it as slow as possible with his baby. However, she wasn't having it. Moet grabbed hold of Harry's 10 inches with both hands and forced as much as she could as deep as she could. Her eyes were closed tightly but when she opened them, Harry was looking directly into them.

He kissed her forehead as he began to slowly move inside of her. He felt the exact moment when his Moet became a woman. His heart was swelling as he continued to move deeper and deeper, losing himself in her sweetness. The juices were threatening to drown them both but they continued to swim. Placing her leg over his shoulder, he traveled to the deepest depths of her ocean.

Moet's body had never felt anything so amazing in her life. The pleasure Harry was giving her right now had her entire body tingling. She held onto his neck and moved in unison as Harry continued to dig deeper in her soul. Moet felt the moment he locked her heart up for good. She was experiencing another eruption; she felt it in her spine. It was so powerful, it caused her to scream out loud.

"Harrrrrrrrrrrrrrrry, oh my god, what are you doing to me!?" Harry continued to dig deeper as her body shook. All the while, looking deep into her soul as he said, "I'm giving you all of me, Moet...everything baby...every part. I love you."

Tears immediately gushed from her eyes as Harry kissed all over her face. He never stopped his pussy assault. However, at that moment, he had his own outburst as he yelled,

"Shiiiiiiiiiit, Mo baby, I'm cummmmmmm, shit!"

His breathing increased as he held on tightly to the one woman who, without even trying, had locked his heart in a vice.

Hours later, they woke up stuck together by the aftermath of their lovemaking. Moet turned slowly, noticing her body was sore yet her heart was happy. She felt like her whole world had changed in merely a couple of hours. For the first time in years, she was happy. It was like everything was in place except the one thing she couldn't change. Harry combed his fingers through her hair with a look of concern as he asked,

"Did I hurt you baby?"

The smile on Moet's face quickly reassured him. Just in case he needed additional assurance, she leaned over and kissed him with so much passion she threatened to start something right back up.

"I'm perfect Harry; I feel amazing right now. I never imagined it would feel like this."

Harry was happy to hear that because he wanted her first time to be special as well as ensure the experience was good for her.

"It makes me feel good that you trusted me like this Moet. I promise to always do right by you." That was all she needed to hear. She kissed him again then lay in his arms and drifted back into a peaceful slumber.

*****

Corey and Eric Bottom were making plans to get back at the bitches who killed their two brothers and had the other unconscious in the hospital. They were aware that once Brandon regained consciousness, he was going straight to jail. Corey was more of an organizer; he wanted to have a game plan to kill Ed and Killa. Additionally, he also wanted that bitch dead. Eric found out that her name is Moet and she's the little cousin of Ed.

Eric was more of their information specialist, there wasn't much he couldn't find out about any situation. The two sat around the table of their Desert Shores estate making plans when their motion detector alarm was tripped. Both men immediately went for their weapons and got into position. Their protocol for if they were ever attacked on their home front was to retaliate not attack. They both sat in the cut as the door slowly crept open. Before they could open fire, they heard something they were not prepared for,

"Alphabet boys, Alphabet boys."

There were only two people other than them that would know that special code, their mother and Brandon. Corey and Eric gave each other a knowing look as Corey yelled back,

"ABCDE."

After hearing the all clear code, Brandon entered the house without fear of being shot on the spot. The brothers shared a manly hug.

They were all glad to see each other. Brandon told his brothers about his escape from the hospital and that Killa and Ed came looking for him. Slamming his hands on the table, fire could be seen in Corey's eyes as he said,

"I want all of their asses dead! It took a month to plan the attack that we just fucked up."

The pain could be heard seeping through Corey as he continued to talk.

"Not only did we lose our brothers, we've made enemies with a lunatic. When we were hired, we gave our assurances."

Standing up quickly and pacing the room, Eric chimed in, "Killa already eliminated the previous team that was sent at him. You're right, we said we could handle it with no problem."

All heads in the room were bobbing up and down when Brandon said, "But we didn't give them a timeframe. Let's plan it again and this time, EVERYBODY dies!" In the meantime, let's put eyes on them niggas and bitches.

*****

Moet and Steph were hanging out in the courtyard on the UNLV campus. The Vegas sun had set and the traffic on campus was slowly thinning out. They were cracking up about the last time they were all together in this very spot laughing at Marisha's silliness. In the last two weeks, they had not spent much time together. Dupree had stepped up to the plate with Steph and was making sure she was okay, in more ways than one.

Moet had been with Harry, who was definitely showing her how deep his love is. Standing up abruptly, Moet gazed across the campus as she said,

"I miss the hell out of her Steph. I just can't stop thinking that shit should have gone differently." Steph nodded her head up and down slowly with a far off look in her eyes as Moet continued.

"Steph, I swear if I don't do something about this, I ain't never gon' be straight. If it weren't for Harry, I wouldn't be holding it together as well as I am."

Steph was on her feet and by Moet's side. She had been feeling this at the core of her heart but hadn't had the opportunity to express it. Touching Moet on the shoulder, Steph said,

"It's consuming me too Mo, but what we gonna do about it? I mean, we could just let the fellas han…" Moet held her hand up, stopping her before she could finish. "Marisha was our girl; we're responsible to bring the heat to the niggas that took her from us. That's real. I don't doubt that Harry, Ed, and Dupree could handle it, but we have to do this for ourselves."

Moet wasn't aware that she was damn near screaming until people were stopping and looking at them. One dude even went as far as to stop and ask if they needed help. But once Moet hit him with a quick mind your fucking business, he hastily moved on.

They both sat back on the bench, permitting silence to overtake them until Steph broke it.

"I'm with you Mo and I may know where we can start."

Steph had Moet's undivided attention now. Steph stood up and placed her hands on her hips as she continued.

"I overheard Dupree talking about some people. He called them the Bottom brothers. He said he was going to personally kill them for killing Marisha and shooting up the spot."

Moet jumped up saying, "Shit." Both girls' hearts were beating fast. Steph continued,

"He didn't know I was listening; I think he thought I was sleeping. Also, he said something about two of the brothers being dead and there being three left."

The two gave each other the beat down look. The one that Marisha was famous for. Moet exclaimed,

"An eye for a fucking eye!"

There was no more that needed to be said; the decision was made and the two friends would do what they needed to avenge their best friend.

Walking to the parking lot, they said their goodbyes and promised to get together the next day to begin planning. Moet had every intention of finding out exactly what the killers at The Lime Light were thinking. It was the key to this entire ordeal.

The Watcher had a good vantage point to see the girls' every move as they sat on the bench in the UNLV courtyard. It was apparent they were in a heated discussion. Their body language gave them away. No matter what they were discussing, The Watcher had already determined today was the day Moet would pay for her sins. As the girls went their separate ways in the parking lot, the grey utility van slowly pulled up beside Moet and the sliding door opened quickly. Before she knew what was happening, Moet was dragged, kicking and screaming into the van. Steph had just started her truck up when she noticed the commotion. What she saw was a grey van speeding away and people pointing in the direction of the screeching tires. When the crowd began to disperse, she noticed Moet's 2004 Mercedes Benz Roadster Convertible was parked in the same spot and Moet was nowhere around. Turning the truck off, she reached for her phone thinking, oh shit, this cannot be happening.

*****

The room smelled of ginger. It was a sweet smell but strong and overpowering. Almost like there was too much of it. She was in arm and leg restraints on a very comfortable bed but she was anything but comfortable. Moet was more pissed than scared. She hated not being in control of her life; it was a feeling she took back from Lecretia years ago. Sadly, now that feeling was back.

The silk blindfold was cutting into her skin as she strained against her restraints in an attempt to free herself. She could feel a light breeze attack her body, she was naked and the ceiling fan was attacking her senses. Moet's brain was on overload with questions. Who snatched me? What do they want? How the fuck am I getting out of this shit? Keys could be heard jingling. Moet decided pretending to be asleep would probably yield her more information. Slowly, the door creaked open and that's when she heard them.

"Good, she's still sleep. That chloroform should be wearing off soon. Did you make the call yet?"

Moet recognized the voice immediately and instantly saw red. It was Superb's punk ass. She wanted to strangle him with her bare hands, but needed to play her position. She had to be smart. Therefore, she closed her eyes tighter, waiting to hear who was in the room with him.

All she could detect was the movement of two people. It sounded like they were moving toward the door then she heard the door slam. Her mind was spinning; she needed to figure out how to get out of this situation. And what call they intended to make? What the fuck? Moet's eyes flew open as she felt someone's hands on her breast. What she saw made her want to throw up.

"I knew your bitch ass wasn't sleep. You think ya ass is slick but ya not." Superb was staring right through Moet. Gone was the look of affection he once had for her. The lustful look he now displayed was mixed with an uncontrollable rage as he continued.

"Ya lil boyfriend is not here to save you this time, Moet. No one is here to baby ya bitch ass. Right now, ya all mine; this pussy is all mine. And I plan on getting my fill of it, I waited long enough."

The scream that came from Moet was deep from a part of her soul she had closed off to the world. She had a pleading look in her eyes as Superb began to lick around her areola.

Moet shook back and forth attempting to free herself from the restraints but to no avail. She had to endure him licking down her body like he was a gentle lover. She could hear him moaning and grunting not believing he was going to actually take her body. Moet felt like a volcano about to erupt. She thought she had moved pass this type of abuse, but here it was once again finding her. When he made it down to her private area, he readjusted himself on the bed and spread her legs apart. Moet immediately closed them but that didn't stop Superb. He forced them open and rammed his dick inside of her as he said,

"I was gonna eat ya pussy, give you something nice but I'm gonna just fuck the shit outta your stuck up ass instead since you wanna play games."

He was pushing himself deeper inside Moet all the while groaning loudly.

"Damn Moet, this is some good fucking pussy. I knew that virgin shit you were claiming was some bullshit. Somebody done been in this pussy already."

Throughout the ordeal, Moet closed her eyes and died a little bit inside. Nevertheless, she was determined to get through it and kill him.

Superb had waited years to fuck Moet. Never did he imagine he would get the pussy under the circumstances he was getting it. Even so, there was no way he was passing up the opportunity to take what he felt he was rightfully due. Recognizing she had already given herself to someone, made his blood boil; he had a good idea who it was. He finished fucking Moet then left her lying in her own juices; he was even more determined to fuck up Harry's life for once again butting into his business. Making his way to the other side of the house, he entered a room that was decorated in a casino theme. If you didn't know you were in a house, you would think you were in a small casino.

There were blackjack, poker, and roulette tables, and even real live slot machines. The color scheme was black and white. A bartender tended a lavishly decorated bar. Superb loved his new life. He got to fuck whenever he wanted to fuck, play blackjack, and plan a big money score. Who could ask for anything more. Sitting at the poker table, Superb chit-chatted with the dealer until The Watcher entered the room.

It was as if everyone came to attention. The atmosphere got more serious. The Watcher approached the poker table and looked him in the face, asking, "So how was the pussy?" Although he knew he was grimy for the shit he was doing, it was still hard for Superb to get with The Watcher's reasons for doing shit, other than the money.

The plan was to get Harry's hood rich ass to pay for the safe return of Moet. Superb believed he would do it too. Conversely, he also comprehended there would be gunplay which is where The Watcher came in. There were hired guns all over the compound, so he knew it wouldn't be easy.

The Watcher moved around the room before answering. "The message will be received today and then the fun begins." Superb was bobbing his head up and down as The Watcher continued. "You might as well get your fill of Moet, 'cause after I get my money, she's done." Superb knew exactly what was meant by that statement but wasn't exactly sure how he felt about it. There was a time when he thought he was in love with Moet. He wasn't entirely sure if he could watch her die. At the same time, he wasn't trying to die. Therefore, it was something to think about.

*****

The Bottom brothers had taken a couple of days to go check on their mother. She was not taking the loss of her boys well. It was as though she didn't even acknowledge what her sons did for a living. She knew very well that they killed someone's son almost daily. Nonetheless, she wouldn't front like she wasn't pissed over losing her own. She told Brandon, Corey, and Eric to get their asses back to Vegas and bury the sons of bitches alive that killed her boys. That was all they needed to hear. They were pulling up to their home.

The Desert Shores neighborhood is not where you would expect to find the Bottom brothers with resort style living, manmade lakes, and bike trails. Their oldest brother Andreas found this neighborhood on the eastern edge of Summerlin. He said it was the perfect cover and exactly how they deserved to live.

The house had six bedroom suites as well as all the amenities. They outfitted the home with surveillance cameras and motion detectors. They never brought people to their house, not even girlfriends. Each of them kept a separate place for that. Desert Shores was for them to relax and plan business. Eric was stretching as he got out of his car. He drove most of the nine hours from Oakland back to Vegas.

Brandon was still not 100% and Corey was only good for about two hours. Before they made it to their door, Metro PD was coming from everywhere. All you could hear was, "Get down...Get on the ground! Metro PD...Get the fuck down now!" The initial shock was over, but they were caught off-guard. There was nothing they could do other than either allow themselves to be taken into custody or end it all right here. Brandon was the first to bend his knees. He gave both of his brothers a look; they too joined him and allowed themselves to be handcuffed. The white people in the neighborhood were holding their chests and pointing like they had never seen shit before.

Vegas Metro PD, Detective Sands walked over to the three men now lying flat on their stomachs with their hands cuffed behind their backs and announced,

"You three are under arrest for the destruction, murder, and mayhem at The Lime Light."

He gave a hard nod to one of the officers who read them the Miranda warning. They were dragged off to separate, undercover police cars.

The brothers watched from the backseats as their home was searched and evidence bags were removed from the house. The media was being held back along with the neighborhood crowd. The entire scene was fucked.

*****

The ringing of the doorbell caused a nervous Toya to jump. Ever since Ed told her that Moet had been snatched off the street, her nerves had been in a knot. Ed and Harry assured her they were doing everything in their power to find Moet, but that didn't make Toya feel any better. Last night, Henry "The Butcher" Blake came to see her. She just called him Henry. It had been years since she had seen him in person. Her husband, Edward, was his right-hand man. Of course, they called him E Dog, but to her he would always be her Edward. Henry was the one who helped her pick up the pieces after her husband died. He took Ed under his wings. Even though she initially objected to the direction Henry was pushing her son in, she didn't stand in their way. It was who her husband was. Perhaps, it's who Ed was as well.

Henry wanted to let Toya know he had his eyes and ears open on the street and that Ed and Harry had his full support. Believe it or not, this actually made Toya feel a little better.

Drying her hands on her apron, she went to see who was ringing her doorbell. She didn't feel up to any visitors. The house was quiet except for the television that had the news blaring. Toya needed the noise of the TV; it was strangely soothing. Somehow, she hoped to hear something about Moet. When she opened the door, no one was there. The sun was blaring and the neighborhood was alive, but her driveway was empty. Stepping outside and closing the door, she saw the white envelope lying on the banister. Toya looked around the neighborhood once again, thinking someone would appear. She merely stood on the porch looking at the envelope, scared to even touch it. Once she opened the letter, she knew there was no turning back.

Ed pulled into his mother's driveway with Harry riding shotgun. They had been following up on leads regarding the Bottom brothers. They found out from a chick who was fucking one of the brothers that they had a hideout crib in the plush, Desert Shores neighborhood. She was also fucking Ed on the low but had dreams of an upgrade. She didn't know Ed had no intentions of serving up more than the dick. Ed turned his music down and parked. The distress was apparent in the worry lines on his forehead. Harry pulled his shades down saying,

"They will bleed for this." Pulling his shades back on his face, they both got out and approached Toya who was still standing on the porch. Immediately, Ed was aware that something was wrong, running toward his mother he said, "What's wrong ma…tell me something!"

Toya grabbed the envelope and walked into the house. She felt more at ease since Ed was home. Ed and Harry followed her into the living room both watching her intensely as she began to open the letter. Ed didn't want to sweat his mother; she didn't like that, but he needed to find out what was going on with her. She looked stressed out. The news caught his attention before he could ask her again what was going on with her. Flores, a Channel 8 anchor, was standing in the Desert Shores neighborhood. The backdrop was yellow tape and undercover cars. The caption read *Lime Light Killers* in custody. Ed and Harry tuned in as Flores spoke.

Today, the scenic Desert Shores neighborhood was rocked by Metro PD as they arrested Bernard, Eric, and Corey Bottom. They are accused of being involved with the massacre at The Lime Light. Police would not confirm. However, sources say their brothers, Andreas and Dante, were among the dead.

There were several patrons killed during this tragedy including Marisha Jones, a 17-year-old recent graduate who was on her way to UNLV.

The report went on to show all of the brothers in the back of police vehicles and police coming out of the home with evidence bags. The reporter also stated other suspects were being sought for questioning. Harry was the first to speak. Taking his shades off and looking at Ed, he said,

"So if they don't have Moet, who snatched my lady?" Ed was pacing in front of the TV scratching his head.

He never noticed his mother come and stand in front of the television, holding a sheet of paper in her hands but Harry did.

"What's wrong Ms. Toya? What do you have there?" Tears were rolling down her face as she said with her voice cracking, "Lecretia has her."

Ed stopped in his tracks and looked at his mother, now realizing what was bothering her. If her stupid ass sister had taken Moet, there was no telling what she had planned.

"Ma, how do you know? What does the letter say?"

Handing Ed the letter, Toya sat in the nearest chair before she fell down. Ed read the letter aloud.

Toya,

The joke is on you FINALLY. You always thought you had it made, had the best, and were better than me. You even thought you could raise my skank ass daughter better than me. Well guess what? You fucked up! E Dog is DEAD, Ed is a killer, and Moet's bitch ass is giving up the pussy like the hoe she is. So now who's the failure? That's what you called me, remember? But enough of the pleasantries. If you want this bitch back alive, then you better tell that nigga she's fucking it's gonna cost him. And tell him don't underestimate me. I'm a bitch with a plan which makes me dangerous. Trust and believe I know what he and Ed did to Bruce. So they need to know I will shoot first and ask questions never if they don't come correct.

What do I want? I'm so glad you asked. Money bitch! That's right, it's always about the all mighty dollar and that big nigga got plenty of it. Shit, he fucking my daughter for free, so I'm entitled, don't you think? Anyway, enough of this bullshit.

Tell Ed's peanut head ass to get $200K from that nigga. I'll contact you and let you know where I want him to bring it. He will come alone, because he and I have some things to talk about. As for you, be thankful you're my sister bitch!

Lecretia (The BITCH y'all love to hate!)

Ed balled the letter up and threw it across the room as he yelled,

"Son of a bitch! I swear I hate that bitch!"

He calmed himself down a little when he saw how distraught his mother was looking. He went to comfort her as Harry picked the letter up and began to reread it.

His features looked different; it was as if he was having an out of body experience. Ed was hugging his mother but he never took his eyes off of Harry.

He realized his friend was hurting; he also knew he was planning to wreak havoc on the city of Vegas. Harry turned to Ed and gave him the look, the one that said someone was about to lose their life. Ed explained to his mother that he wouldn't come back without Moet.

Toya nodded her head in agreement then stood abruptly, stopping both of them in their tracks as she said in a voice that belied her actual anguish, but didn't hide the hatred she was feeling,

"Lecretia is a poison. She always has been. She was that way when we were kids and carried it into her adulthood. It's time for it to end."

The look she revealed didn't hide her meaning at all as she looked each of them in their eyes separately. Harry gave her a strong head nod and Ed winked, letting her know he understood exactly what she wanted him to do. Toya watched as they left her home with assurances that she would contact them as soon as she got a meeting place from Lecretia.

She was pissed at herself, thinking this is my fault. I should have dealt with her ass after she killed my husband years ago. A new rage was building in Toya as the memories began to flood back.

Dressed in a black Gucci dress that her mother picked out for her, Toya was sitting in the church still trying to wrap her head around the fact that he was gone. Edward had been everything to her since she was 15-years-old. In a world where she didn't feel pretty, loved, or protected, he filled that void. She was left with memories, and an 18-year-old son who was the spitting image of him from toe to head. As she contemplated what she would do with the rest of her life and how she would be able to be there for her son, her sister sat down beside her.

Immediately, Toya got a headache. Although she was happy her sister came to pay her respect, she didn't feel like dealing with her theatrics today. Toya was well aware that if the spotlight was not on Lecretia, she wouldn't make it through the day without directing attention her way.

Lecretia cleared her throat, causing Toya to cut her eyes in her direction. Lecretia was dressed in a hip hugging, red dress that was not appropriate for a funeral, but that was Lecretia. She just didn't give a fuck.

She smiled at Toya and said,

"This is all his fault you know."

She ignored the surprised look on her sister's face as she continued.

"If he would have just given me what I asked him for, he might still be alive."

Toya jumped up from her seat, ready to tear a hole in her sister's ass. But was floored by her next statement,

"I called the police and informed on E Dog. All I asked his selfish ass was for some money and some of that monster he had in his pants. Because of your ass, he refused to give me either. Well now you don't even have it."

With that last statement, Lecretia attempted to get up but Toya jumped on her like she was a member of the WWF. She punched, kicked, and scratched all the time yelling,

"You are not my sister...You are not my sister!"

Her mother tried to pull them apart but was pushed by Lecretia as she tried to retaliate against a still swinging Toya. It took Henry, Ed, and Harry to pry Toya's hands from around Lecretia's throat. Toya was actually trying to kill her.

When she was saved from the grips of death, Lecretia didn't let well enough alone. Instead, through loud coughs, she yelled at the top of her lungs,

"Fuck all of y'all! I hate you bitches! And fuck E Dog's bitch ass too!" That last statement sent Ed into a downward spiral.

He punched Lecretia in her face and was about to attack her when his grandmother dragged a bloody, screaming, Lecretia out of the church.

Still standing in the same spot, Toya was jarred from that painful memory by the sound of children playing outside. With a heavy heart, she reflected on never telling Henry or even Ed what the fight in the church was really about. She understood that if The Butcher knew Lecretia was behind the raid, she would be dead in a matter of days. Plus, Toya was worried about Moet. Moving around the house keeping her nerves at bay, it saddened her that she was still not able to protect Moet. But this was the last straw. Lecretia had to go. She had hurt this family for the last time. Toya was finally ready to release that demon from her life, thinking maybe now Edward can finally rest in peace. The ringing of her phone caused her to jump.

*****

Superb was perspiring uncontrollably as he continued to assault a subdued Moet. She was present in the room but her soul had left already; she refused to give that to him too. While he was still deep inside of her, talking in her ear as if this continuous rape was a consensual act, he said something that caused her rage to overflow. Pounding deep inside of her, not affected by her lack of feeling or the dryness of her sex, he said,

"You Rollins women got some good pussy. Your momma's shit is good but nothing compares to this shit." Moet's eyes popped open. She knew she heard him right.

Had Superb slept with Lecretia? She questioned herself. Moet decided she needed to find out what the fuck was going on. She made a pact with herself to use herself, not be used. Instead of laying catatonic while he pumped relentlessly into her, Moet began to move beneath him and use her muscles to grab hold of his dick. Her juices began to flow and his moaning increased. He was moaning so loud and dripping so much sweat into Moet's eyes, she was sure she would go both death and blind. Just as he was about to release his seed in her, he stunned Moet by whispering in her ear that he loved her.

Still lying on top of Moet as his breathing regulated, Superb began whispering,

"Why you fuck that nigga, Mo? Why you throw us away like that? You think I wanted you like this? But you let that nigga play me in front of everybody. I can't believe you did that to me." Moet could detect he was becoming emotional.

Despite the fact that she wanted to cuss him from night to day, she played it cool by saying,

"I didn't know he would do that. You can't think I wanted that. How long have we been together? I wasn't dating anyone but you. I didn't give anything to anyone. It was taken from me, just like you're taking it now. Seems like that's all y'all want to do is hurt me."

When Moet made that statement, it was like something switched in Superb. He jumped up from her yelling,

"That nigga rapped you, Mo!?" He was pacing back and forth. "What the fuck! I'm gonna kill this nigga, Mo! Do you understand me? Man fuck what yo momma talking about. I want this nigga dead." Moet saw her opportunity to get a better understanding, so she said, "Me too Superb. I'm tired of being under his thumb." She let the tears flow down her face.

It was the first time she had cried since being held captive. She refused to let him see her vulnerable. Once he saw the tears fall, he knew she was telling the truth. This changed some things for Superb but he knew Lecretia wasn't trying to hear it.

*****

Lecretia sat in her leather recliner staring out the window at nothing in particular. Her emotions were all over the place. She never gave a fuck how people viewed her; she either got what she wanted or others would pay the price, it was as simple as that.

When Moet fucked up her smooth ride with Bruce and put the law onto her, Lecretia fled Vegas and ended up in California.

She was a fresh faced beauty with elegance and charm. It was easy for her to maneuver her way into the right bed. She was introduced to Jorge "J.D." Dundes at a black tie function. She assumed he was a wealthy businessman but once she discovered he controlled the dope pipeline between California and Nevada, she was hooked. JD was captivated by Lecretia's beauty in the streets and definitely in the sheets. They became inseparable and had been married for the last two years.

Throughout their marriage Lecretia never wanted for anything, except to make the people who ran her out of Vegas pay. She had her chance when she overheard J.D. on the phone discussing money issues with his business partner. He was concerned about the level of drugs that were being seized. Thereby, costing them. Therefore, he wanted to find an alternative revenue stream. Typically, Lecretia didn't make her snooping obvious, but she felt like she needed to make a grand entrance. She walked in the room looking stunning as usual, which normally put J.D. in a good mood. This time, he was upset saying sternly,

"Lecretia, you know I'm not to be disturbed when I'm talking business."

Sashaying over to her husband she responded,

"I know honey and you know I normally don't, but I know a way to help you increase your revenue."

J.D. told his partner he would call him back then turned back to Lecretia. Before he could say anything she said,

"All I need is 10 of your best killers and a couple of weeks."

That was four weeks ago. She had years to brood over what she wanted to do to Moet, Ed, and Toya. Over the years, she had travelled to Vegas many times on business trips with her husband which is when she first started watching. She was following Bruce the night that Ed and Harry kicked in the door of his hotel room.

At first, she didn't know who Harry was but that quickly changed. With more research, she found out about his father, their money, and hotels. Additional observation provided her with the information that Harry was smitten with Moet. It showed in the way he stared at her. She didn't approach Superb until after she saw him get beat down at the graduation party. Lecretia recognized the pretty boy was ripe for the picking. Thus, she recruited him due to his anger. She even seduced him. It was the only way she could totally turn him against Moet. The plan that formulated in her head was to ransom Moet, kill her, and then disappear back to California.

Rising from her chair and walking over to the well-stocked mini bar she deduced that Superb would have to die as well. Shaking her head she thought to herself, what a waste, the young boy had some good dick.

She had already placed the call to Toya's bitch ass to let her know where and how the exchange would take place. The second part of her plan was to kill Ed, yet again, taking something from Toya. She didn't want to kill Toya; she wanted her to suffer the loss of those closest to her. Her plan was to wrap this up and be back in Cali before morning.

The loud crash coming from the lobby got Lecretia's attention. She had J.D.'s men surrounding the small villa. She wasn't worried about Ed and Harry getting in without some gunplay. When she looked up, what she saw startled her. There in a soiled bed sheet wrapped around her Egyptian style was Moet. A fire burned in her eyes that said she was not there to listen nor give an apology. In her hand was a .357 Magnum. Lecretia bursting into laughter only further fueled Moet's anger. The first bullet that tore through Lecretia's right shoulder knocked her off her feet and definitely put an end to the cackling. Moet was way beyond anger at this point. All the memories of the hatred her mother had for her surfaced. Moet didn't even want answers; aiming the gun, she shot Lecretia in her left leg. At this point, Lecretia was crying, bleeding, and begging. Moet wasn't trying to hear any of it as she said,

"I've been crying for you to be a mother since the day I was born. I'm your blood but that didn't matter to you. You allowed men to misuse me, rape me, rip my fucking heart out, so the begging means absolutely nothing to me."

By now, Moet was going through so many emotions but the most important one was satisfaction. She aimed the gun at her mother's head and asked one thing, "Why?"

Lecretia was shaking, possibly going into shock. She knew her time was limited, but before she left this earth, she was going to do one honest thing. Glaring at her daughter, flesh of her flesh, the disgust remained present as she declared through the pain,

"I hated you before you were born. You remind me of the darkest days of my life. The day when my innocence was stolen from me and nobody gave a fuck."

She spit blood as she locked eyes with Moet and continued.

"No one cared that my life was destroyed. All they wanted to do was make sure you were ok. No one cared that my daddy is my baby's father. Even though I told them, they refused to believe me and made me feel like shit the entire nine months that your demon ass was growing in my belly. Shit got so bad that I started to believe I deserved the pain. Then one day, I decided that you deserved it too. So there you have it, you're the product of my daddy raping me and I can't stand the sight of you."

The revelation didn't surprise Moet. In contrast, she refused to allow herself to feel anything for the woman who had made her life a living hell.

Before she pulled the trigger, she said,

"But I was your child. You should have protected me, like you were not protected. But you didn't so the penalty for that is death." With that, she pulled the trigger and sent Lecretia to meet her maker, whomever that is.

*****

When Lecretia made the call to Toya, she didn't know that Harry, Ed, Dupree, and Steph were already on that side of Summerlin. They used Steph as a distraction with her broke down car then each guard was systematically taken out. By utilizing silenced weapons, they went undetected. Moving through the villa, they encountered about four more guards who were also cut down before they could mount a defense. Harry was in Killa mode. His team was efficient and on point. They went room by room silently opening doors, still maintaining the element of surprise.

When they came to the last room in the hallway and Harry opened the door, his heart immediately exploded in his chest. He saw the love of his life spread across a bed naked with her arms and legs bound. She was asleep and didn't hear him approach; he heard someone in the bathroom. Without even giving it a second thought, Harry began to fire through the door. Bullet after bullet entered it. As a result, whoever was on the other side was surely dead.

The commotion woke a sore and sleepy Moet who quickly sat up as far as she could. What she saw caused her to open the floodgates that had been held back. Harry was standing over her with such an expression of anxiety and hurt bearing down on his soul that it literally broke her heart as he declared,

"Baby, I'm here. I'm so sorry baby...I'm so sorry!"

Moet shushed him as he released her from her bondage. Harry had to pick her up from the bed. She had been lying in one spot for so long her body was severely sensitive. Harry wrapped her in a sheet from the bed just as Ed came bursting into the room. When he saw his cousin, his heart felt heavy.

"Moet, oh my god; I fucking can't believe this shit!"

He was staring at the open bathroom door where Superb was lying on the bathroom floor with several holes in his chest and head. Just then, Moet spoke with a raspy voice in a confident tone that under the circumstances she was surprised she had. "Lecretia is behind this. She's here. Give me a gun." Moet held out her hand as both Ed and Harry were handing her a gun.

*****

Moet spent three weeks in the hospital. She was subject to every kind of test known to man; she was ready to go home. Harry and Ed spent almost every waking minute in the hospital. The night before she was scheduled to be released, she woke up to Harry sitting on her bed.

He looked so handsome, a breath of fresh air. He had a serious look in his eyes that Moet was tuned into as he said,

"Hey baby, I wanted to talk to you before you left."

Moet sat up in the bed. Harry took her hands in his and rubbed them as he continued to speak,

"I love you Moet. Almost losing you nearly caused me to go insane."

While reaching in his pocket, he never broke eye contact with her. He held a Tiffany ring box in his hand and conveyed,

"I want to always be there to protect you Moet. I need to show you how someone is supposed to love you. I need you to make me better. Please baby. Please be my wife."

He extended his hand toward her cheek to wipe away some of the tears cascading from her eyes. She attempted to speak but through the tears all he could make out was yes.

They Got Me Fucked Up! (Present Day)

The annoying buzzing sound jarred Moet back to reality.
She was still on the kitchen floor clutching the phone in
her hand. Her current state made her realize she had not
been dreaming; her husband and son were truly dead.
With a dry throat and her ears ringing, continuing to cry
was not an option. She didn't think she had any tears left.
What Moet was left with was a tightness in her chest and
vengeance in her heart. Determined not to be a victim,
she picked herself up off the floor; she wanted fucking
answers! Moet moved swiftly through the house, heading
for her husband's study. It was still early in the day, but
before she dealt with anything else, she was determined
to know what the fuck was going on.

The alert sounding through the house demanded her
attention. She pulled up the outside surveillance monitors
in her husband's study and immediately stood at
attention. What she saw were at least five men with
assault rifles closing in on her home. Instantly, she hit the
red button at the bottom of her husband's desk then the
wall on the opposite side of the room parted like the red
sea. Running to the room, she began to arm herself. All
the time thinking,

"These bitches must think it's a game. Kill my husband.
Kill my son. Come for me. Naw that Moet died a long
time ago. You got the right one baby." She was the only
one who could hear the venom of her words.

Nevertheless, she meant every one of them. Killa made sure Moet was fully trained with almost every weapon known to man. He knew the time would come when someone would try her again simply because she was his wife. The first time she picked up a gun again after killing her mother, was a little different. No one knew her like her husband though; he put his arms around her waist and whispered in her ear that there was nothing sexier than a bad bitch with a killa shot. It's funny now, but that's all it took for her to become the marksman she is today. Moet lived to make her man proud of her. Once HJ was born, Killa continued to stress the importance of always being ready for bullshit. Hence; Moet was always packing.

There was a loud explosion coming from the front of her home. In broad daylight, these muthafuckas coming for me. Moet thought as she made her way to a strategic place in the room. Whoever entered was going straight to hell. She pulled out her cell and put it on vibrate while she sent a quick text to Ed with the distress code that Killa set up.

MOE. MOE. ASAP 911

Moet could hear slight movement coming from the bottom of the house. She closed her eyes and concentrated; she wanted to feel the danger as it got closer. Her phone vibrated in her pocket. Looking at the phone it was a text alert from Ed.

MOE. MOE 10 minutes out. Hold on MOET

Placing the phone back in her pocket, she knew her boys were on their way to blow operation kill Moet all the way up. However, before they got there, she planned on taking a couple of them straight to hell her damn self.

There was movement near the door; she could hear whispering. Moet remembered that Killa always told her to be patient and let the kill come to her. Observing from her hiding spot and perched in her killing stance, three men made their way into the room and spread out. They wore army fatigues, each toting semiautomatic firepower. There was nothing special about their appearance and she didn't recognize them. The taller of the men appeared to be the leader and was pointing around the room directing traffic. The men searched but were unable to locate Moet.

The frustration level was growing as the leader got a message over his earbud and promptly slammed his hand on the desk saying,

"The bitch ain't here! Find the safe and let's get the fuck outta here!"

That was it for Moet. She could hardly breathe; she wanted to make them bleed so badly. Without another moment's hesitation, she appeared like a thief in the night, aiming her MK II with a silencer, dropping all three men with quick precision before they even had the opportunity to return fire. Her Ruger is her favorite .22 and has never let her down. Just then, she heard a huge boom and a lot of return fire, alerting her that MOE was in the house.

Moet didn't join the gunfight. Instead, she went through the pockets of each body as the grim reaper was leaving with their souls. She needed to have more information about who these men were and who sent them.

Ed, Tony, Dupree, and Clevon came bursting in the room with their guns at the ready. They stopped dead in their tracks when they saw all of the dead bodies sprawled out on the floor and Moet sitting behind Killa's desk with her feet up and her .22 in her hands.

Ed was the only one in the room who knew Moet was good with a pistol. Tony, Dupree, and Clevon all looked from the bodies to Moet then the biggest smiles creased their lips.

Ed made his way to Moet and sat on the edge of the desk. His main purpose at that very moment was to ensure his lil cousin was ok. Today had been the worst day of her life, and all he wanted to do was help her through it. He scratched his beard and looked out the window behind the desk and said,

"The house is clean. Problem neutralized. But they'll be back." Moet acknowledged him with a head nod as he continued, "What you wanna do cuz?"

Everyone in the room was looking at her. They could see the fury in her eyes as well as the hate on her face. Moet knew she wanted the bitches that took her life away from her to cease to exist; she wanted their head on her wall. And that's exactly what she said as she looked each man in their eyes, "I want them all dead!"

Vindication

He sat in his darkened living room with no music, TV, or sound to keep him company. He was waiting for a phone call that would change his life. He wanted to know that the job was done. He had waited a long time to bring destruction to the people who had ripped his heart from its place and left only hurt and pain. Deciding long ago he would wait to exact his vengeance; he bided his time until they were deep in their success, until they had something to lose. Five long years he watched them go on with their lives while despite his success his life had changed forever. From the outside, he watched them continue to do their dirt underground. Now it was time to pay the piper and today was collection day.

The ringing phone interrupted his thoughts but made his heart leap for joy. Snatching it off the receiver much harder than he intended, he said in a hollow voice,

"Tell me!" Listening to the initial report, a sinister smile crept to the corner of his mouth. As the caller continued, that smile morphed into outrage as he yelled,

"What do you mean they didn't kill her! It's one bitch! How the fuck she kill five, well-armed niggas!?"

Shaking his head at the dumb explanations coming from the other end of the phone, he was growing angrier by the second. No one understood how deep his hurt and pain went.

Trying to gather as much composure as he could, he spoke in a calm monotone voice,

"Get that bitch and I mean do it now!"

Having said that, he slammed the phone down and stared at the painting on the wall, vowing he would be vindicated.

Down to Business

Hanging from the ceiling in the musty smelling warehouse were the Bottom brothers, Brandon, Corey, and Eric. The chain was cutting into one of the brother's skin and threatened to rip through his wrist. There was an odor to the old warehouse; it was a cross between stale urine and perspiration. The men standing around the room were all heavily armed, resembling your typical bodyguards. Their necks were thick and their faces held permanent scowls. On the contrary, there was nothing typical about the firepower in the room or the men that displayed it. Only the Kings of the Jungle could stand guard in MOE. Four of them were in the center of the room standing guard, but there were five others you couldn't find with a microscope; who were ensuring the safety of the package. What they were guarding was very important; they were cautioned to protect the merchandise with their lives.

The clicking on the cement floor sounded like an exaggerated ticking clock. The closer the sound got, the more alert the men in the room became. They were standing at attention as she made her final approach. And what an approach it was. Each man in the room did his very best to remember she was the Bawss. However, it was difficult to overlook her beauty; it was one of her best weapons. It distracted the weakest of men and confused the best of them. She was deadly by design; Killa refused to have it any other way.

Noticing that her men were on point as usual, she tilted her Versace shades to get a better look at the package. The Bottom brothers she thought to herself as she shook her head from side-to-side with a sinister grin forming in the corner of her mouth. It was time to guarantee that Vegas not only received the message but got it clearly. If you wanted to dance with the devil, you would discover for certain that the devil really does wear Prada.

Moet watched the Bottom brothers for a moment longer before she spoke. Her voice was authoritative but not forceful.

"So it turns out that the men who broke into my house today belonged to you."

It didn't take long for Ed to find out who sent the team of killers to Moet.

The men were dangling from the rafters. They wore identical cryptic expressions. They were not easy men to get the drop on, but they knew the game which meant they were prepared to die. They were released from prison after 5 years but still had an unpaid debt. They remained the best wet team in Nevada. Their reputation was legendary and they only took on high profile cases. Killa and Moet Blake were explosive. In less than 24 hours, she had turned the tables on them.

Jimmy Choo emerald printed stilettos added another four inches to her 5'4" frame. The weight of the 9mm Glock 26 added to her attitude. Moet learned a long time ago to shoot first and ask questions never.

Therefore, the sound of the bullet leaving the chamber was not a surprise to anyone in the room other than the Bottom brothers. Brandon Bottom reluctantly winced in pain as the bullet entered his left shoulder. The smoke from her Glock dissipated as Moet said,

"The next one goes in your head."

She pointed the pistol toward Eric, providing him with a devious smirk.

"I want to know who sent you to destroy my family." Before they could fully digest her comment, the back of Corey's head exploded. Smoke was still coming from Moet's Glock as she pointed it at Brandon and said,

"I'm only going to ask once."

Ed was standing next to Dupree, beaming with pride. He realized this was difficult for Moet. Nonetheless, she was handling it just like Killa would have wanted her to. An hour earlier, she had to attempt to identify the bodies of her loved ones. Sadly, they were burned so badly she couldn't recognize the two loves of her life. Ed watched her stand in that autopsy room and turn to steel. He grieved with her. In Killa, he lost a brother. Losing HJ in the middle of all of this was devastating to everyone involved.

The thunderous sound coming from Moet's weapon would get the hardest man's attention. As Brandon witnessed his last brother die, he shot daggers at the bitch who had stolen his entire family. It was like Moet could read his mind as she said,

"Yes, that's exactly what it feels like. You guys stole my entire family from me. And if you don't want me to make a special trip to Oakland and visit dear old mom, you better tell me what the fuck I wanna know."

Aiming her weapon at him, she could almost see the wheels turning in his head.

Brandon hung his head low and decided to make a deal with the devil. He was aware that he was a dead man regardless. He merely wanted the certainty that his mother's life would be spared. With that thought, he looked Moet in her eyes and said,

"We were originally hired by your mother. We had a job to do. We're from California and the Dundes crew are heavy hitters. Your mother was married to the kingpin, Jorge Dundes. He found her journal; he knew that she hired us and we botched the initial hit. He sent word that we were obligated to complete the contract or we would all be taken out along with our mom."

Moet listened intently. Right before she pulled the trigger and sent Brandon to his heaven or hell she said,

"So Jorge Dundes is the man I need to kill?"

The question was rhetorical; there was no need for a reply. In fact, the whistle from her pistol as the bullet left it and entered Brandon's head was answer enough.

Be on the look- out Moet's Revenge?....

Coming Soon From Blaque Diamond
Publications!

Part 2 to the Moet Story!

Moet's Revenge

Lust and Love are in a tug of war in this tale of a marriage stretched to its limit.

Meet Briann Jennings, CEO of Glamour Girl Inc., an unapologetic independent woman, but how long will she continue to let the demons of her past dictate her future?

Enter Jason Matthews, owner of JM Advertising, tall dark and handsome; every woman's dream and the envy of all his boys; but has he met his match in Briann?

Hudson Duke, heir to the Beauty Mark throne, is trying to out run his families' secrets while he hides his passion for another man's wife.

Lies and Deceit threaten to cause cracks in this marriage as everyone wants in and no one wants out

About The Author

Born and raised in Oakland California, Fanita Pendleton relocated to Norfolk Virginia during her senior year in high school, and has called the magnificent city home ever since. Fanita began her career as a Juvenile Probation Officer and later worked in Adult Probation before taking a short break to pursue her love of teaching as a Criminal Justice Instructor at a local technical college. Recently Fanita stepped back into law enforcement, and is now a Parole Officer.

Fanita blazed on the scene with her Criminal Romance Series: Shoot First Ask Questions Never, Fist Full of Tears, Fist Full of Tears: The Sequel, The Moscato Diaries, Act Like A Lady, Think Like A Boss: Vegas…MOET: Money Over Everything. An avid reader, Fanita holds a special place in her heart for the unsung genre of Urban Crime and Urban Romance Dramas, and in her youth, devoured the works of such greats as Donald Goines, and Iceberg Slim. She is an author with SBR Publications and a card carrying member of The Bank Roll Squad #TBRS Family. Fanita is Owner of Blaque Diamond Publications an Urban Moon Productions company where she is now giving young authors their shot at making their dreams come true.

Fanita received her Masters' Degree in Public Administration from Troy University, as well as a Bachelors in Sociology from Langston University, and her Associates in Communications from Luzerne County

Community College. She enjoys shooting pool, both for league and leisure, and catching a football, or basketball game with her son, the inspiration of her dreams. Connect with Fanita on Facebook "Fanita Moon Pendleton", Instagram #FanitaPendleton, Twitter @Moon081471 or through her website http://www.urbanmoonproductions.com

Currently Available from Blaque Diamond Publications an Urban Moon Productions Company

Tales of A Plus Size Diva: Lillian's Story by Shauntrell Perry

Tales of A Plus Size Diva Part 2 by Shauntrell Perry

Justifiable Insanity by Jauwel

Self Made Bitch by Jauwel

Self Made Bitch 2 by Jauwel

A Daughters Rage by Roni J.

A Daughter's Rage Part 2: Mona's Revenge by Roni J.

Diary of A Hood Princess by K.L. Hall

Diary of A Hood Princess Part 2 by K.L. Hall

Diary of A Hood Princess Part 3 by K.L. Hall

Taste Like Kandi by Keita B

Taste Like Kandi 2 by Keita B

FML: Fuck My Life by Mimi Ray

FML: Fuck My Life Part 2 by Mimi Ray

FML: Fuck My Life Part 3 by Mimi Ray

The Triple Cross: Love Is Not A Game by Mimi Ray

I Am That Bitch by Cinnamon Brown

I Am That Bitch 2 by Cinnamon Brown

I Am That Bitch 3 by Cinnamon Brown

Our Babies Daddy by Cinnamon Brown

Our Babies Daddy 2 by Cinnamon Brown

The Moscato Diaries by Fanita Moon Pendleton

Never Bite The Hand That Feeds You by Cashmeout

Never Bite The Hand That Feeds You Part 2 by
Cashmeout

Act Like A Lady, Think Like A Boss: Vegas by Fanita
Pendleton, K.L. Hall, Shauntrell Perry

Act Like A Lady, Think Like A Boss: Baltimore by Mimi
Ray and Keita B

Act Like A Lady, Think Like A Boss: Miami by Mimi
Ray and Jauwel

Love Don't Love Nobody by Sweet Pea

Love Don't Love Nobody 2: The Seed by Sweet Pea

Chaos: Life As We Know It by Shanard Smith

Loving A Baller by Chantel Sills

<u>Coming Soon from Blaque Diamond Publications an</u>

<u>Urban Moon Productions Company</u>

Tales of a Plus Size Diva Part 3 by Shauntrell Perry

Justifiable Insanity Part 2 by Jauwel

Self Made Bitch Part 3 by Jauwel

Taste Like Kandi Part 3 by Keita B

A Daughter's Rage Part 3 by Roni J.

Loyal 2 a G by Roni J.

Mocha: The Ultimate Sacrifice by Meka

The Triple Cross: Love Is Not A Game 2 by Mimi Ray

Loving A Baller 2 by Chantel Sills

Unbreakable by Keita B

Love Don't Love Nobody 3 by Sweet Pea

Chaos: Life As We Know It Part 2 by Shanard Smith

Moet's Revenge by Fanita Pendleton

Moscato Diaries 2 by Fanita Pendleton

If you have a manuscript you would like us to review and/or want to be placed on the BDP Newsletter list, email us at:

Blaquediamondpublications@gmail.com

Visit our Facebook Fan Page at Blaque Diamond Publications.